FATE'S DEMAND

ALEATHA ROMIG

NEW YORK TIMES BESTSELLING AUTHOR

A dark-romance short story

New York Times, Wall Street Journal, and USA Today bestselling author of the Consequences series, Infidelity series, and Sparrow Webs: Web of Sin, Tangled Web, Web of Desire, and Dangerous Web

COPYRIGHT AND LICENSE
INFORMATION

FATE'S DEMAND

Copyright @ 2021 Romig Works, LLC
Published by Romig Works, LLC
2021 Edition
ISBN: 978-1-947189-78-2
Cover art: Letitia Hasser – RBA Designs
Editing: Lisa Aurello
Formatting: Romig Works, LLC

This is a work of fiction. Names, characters, places, and incidents either are the product of the author's imagination or are used fictitiously, and any resemblance to any actual persons, living or dead, events, or locales is entirely coincidental.

2021 Edition License

This e-book is licensed for your personal enjoyment. This ebook may not be resold or given away to other people. If you would like to share this book with another person, please purchase an additional copy for each recipient. If you're reading this book and did not purchase it, or it was not purchased for your use only, then please return to the appropriate retailer and purchase your own copy. Thank you for respecting the hard work of this author.

NOTE FROM ALEATHA

"FATE'S DEMAND" first appeared in the Bookworm Box anthology *ONE MORE STEP* as a short story entitled "THE DEAL." For the Bookworm Box anthology, each author was given an opening sentence and asked to create a story that represents their unique writing style.

As "THE DEAL" took shape, it became obvious to me that I needed more Rett and Emma in my life. Their story took place in the lust-filled world of New Orleans, the perfect setting for intrigue, mystery, and dangerous romance.

I knew immediately that I needed more than a short story. I hope you feel the same way after reading the re-titled story, "FATE'S DEMAND."

If you do, I hope you'll read *DEVIL'S DEAL*

coming in May of 2021...knowing it all began with fate's demand.

Enjoy Rett and Emma's first meeting.

-Aleatha

"FATE'S DEMAND"

Stepping into the city limits, the vibes of New Orleans infiltrate the thoughts and feelings of each unsuspecting individual.

Twinkling lights.

Copious amounts of alcohol.

And

Ghost stories of lore.

As Emma waits for a business meeting, those ingredients are there, in the heavy air and circulating through her bloodstream. Until everything changes.

Everett Ramses is tall, dark, and mysterious.

He's more than that.

According to him...he is Emma's fate.

And he has a demand.

Will she run, or will she find out what fate's demand has in store?

"FATE'S DEMAND" is an intriguing meeting to whet readers' appetite for more of an all-new dark-romance world by New York Times bestselling author Aleatha Romig. Get ready to love and hate, to swoon and swear...Rett Ramses will bring out all the emotions.

"FATE'S DEMAND" first appeared in the Bookworm Box anthology ONE MORE STEP as a short story entitled "THE DEAL."

CHAPTER ONE

"*...One* more step would mean certain death."

My blue eyes opened wide. Goose bumps prickled my skin, and my stomach churned with the wine I'd recently consumed.

I reached for the back of the chair, my legs unsteady, and contemplated my next move as past uncertainties came to sudden light.

Was I facing my new life, or was I doomed to die?

CHAPTER TWO
EARLIER

*S*uch a vague time frame—earlier.
An hour?
A week?
A month?

How far back would I need to go to see clues or traps that had been laid, leading to this undeniable precipice in my life?

How could I determine what was wrong or right?

Was correctness something one learned in infancy or perhaps early childhood?

Who were the teachers?

What if the teachers who imparted wisdom to a young mind were deceitful in their mission?

As a young girl, my family would vacation along the sandy white beaches of Florida's west coast. My not-much-older brother and I would build sandcastles, complete with towers and moats, both of us running to and from the shore to collect buckets of water before our hard work seeped into the sand, leaving our moat less of a water deterrent and more of a wet sand trap.

For years we ran into the warm, salty water without hesitation, and then one day while turning channels on our television in the North Carolina mountains, we heard the daunting music and watched as a giant shark maliciously hunted three men who were on a boat that was too small.

The next vacation, the two of us stood, hand in hand, peering out over the once-fun crystal-blue water, certain that within its depths a predator lurked. It was then that our mother pointed to the buoys spaced what seemed like yards apart, creating a straight line. We'd seen them before but never thought much about them.

"What you can't see," she said as she pointed from one to the other, connecting the dots, "are the nets beneath the water. Big nets. They keep the sharks away."

"But," my brother—the older and wiser one—said, "there have been dolphins on this side."

"Yes," she replied, "they can jump over. Sharks can't."

Suddenly, the water was again welcoming.

CHAPTER 2

It wasn't until years later when we were much better swimmers that we learned of her deception. The water was warm as we raced to the sandbar and beyond. Our finish line was the mysterious buoys in the distance.

Seconds ahead of me, Kyle's hand reached the white metal of the buoy.

I too reached out, my breathing labored as we both laughed until we didn't...the same thought occurring in each of our minds simultaneously.

Our feet kicked, keeping us afloat as we circled. The floating object was attached to a chain with large links. In the clear gulf water, we saw the large anchor below. What we didn't see was the net.

It didn't exist.

When confronted, our mother claimed to not recall telling us such a far-fetched tale.

That was the way it was with false truths—they were difficult to remember and maintain unless you lived them day in and day out.

So where to begin this story...the day I was adopted into a family that I was raised to believe was my own, the day when my family was tragically lost, or maybe the day I learned that they weren't my family at all? Or perhaps that was history, and I should start with more recent events...

CHAPTER THREE
EARLIER IN THE EVENING

Tourists sipped colorful drinks and swayed to the sound of jazz as white lights twinkled above the courtyard. This wasn't my scene. I was only here because of the man across the table from me. He wasn't my date or even my friend but my business partner. There was a time we may have been friends, but that was before. Ross Underwood and I met our junior year at the University of Pittsburgh, both majoring in English literature. We believed in the promise for our future.

Handsome and determined, Ross was the kind of guy who caught every woman's eye. In our department, the two of us were constantly at odds, both vying for valedictorian. Ross was going to be a famous editor, sought after by a big New York publisher. Me, my plans included writing. I walked into libraries and bookstores, inhaling the scent of paper and books, imagining my name upon the covers. I didn't want to be just present on a shelf near the back of the store but front and center on the round table near the entry, showcased for the world to see.

It seemed that as much as Ross and I claimed our differences, we shared the same dream—New York. We weren't alone; it was also the goal of every other literature major in the country.

Finally graduated and still living in Pittsburgh, Ross and I came to the conclusion that success could be best met if we combined our strengths.

It should be said that at no time were either of us romantically interested in one another. It wasn't that Ross wasn't handsome—he was—or that I wasn't what some consider pretty, I was. It was that Ross had a problem. There were other women I knew who made the mistake of dating him. Ross was many things when it came to business—determined, intelligent, and resourceful.

As a boyfriend, he was shit.

Perhaps due to his infidelity in relationships, I shouldn't have trusted him as a business partner. Then again, he was honest about his lack of monogamy, truthful not only with me but also with each woman he dated.

His honesty didn't matter. Each woman went into the relationship with stars in her eyes, determined to be the one to change his ways.

Ross wasn't going to change.

He would conquer the world and reach incredible heights in business, not in a personal relationship. The only thing he was true to was attaining success. In that I believed.

Sipping a Hurricane cocktail as Ross rambled on about the possibility of our newest creation, my mind was on anyone and anything except him. The air was sweltering as more bodies made their way into the courtyard. The tall walls surrounding us on all sides obstructed any possibility of a breeze as the live band played their New Orleans sound.

It wasn't that I didn't care about what Ross was saying. I did. It was that we'd picked over this subject to death. Over and over we'd worked. For months at home, hours on the airplane...I was done.

The premise we'd created brought our knowledge and skills to the common writer for a cost. The world of big publishing houses was on life support, the ice caps melting and forests burning. Even some of the biggest names in fiction were turning their backs on the very publishers who years and decades ago had made them into household names. The news outlets were bubbling with stories as renowned authors secured multimillion-dollar deals, working directly with the biggest online distributor of—well, everything. Self-publishing was on the rise in exponential terms, and Ross and I were poised to break into that market.

Our editing program would revolutionize self-publishing. It was unlike any other available…

I swirled the straw in the last few sips of the peach-colored liquid. The ice cubes rattled as Ross's monologue reached its crescendo, and my body swayed to the alluring sound of jazz.

"…this could be it, our answer." Ross reached across the table. "Emma, are you even listening?"

"Yes, and I've heard it all…" *a million times*. I didn't say the last part. "Save it for this mysterious Mr. Ramses." I shivered as the name left my lips—Everett Ramses. Maybe it wasn't his name that caused my reaction but just being in New Orleans where ghost stories abounded, or perhaps it was the alcohol coursing through my bloodstream minus food I should have eaten.

"Em," Ross said, "the man has more capital than you or I could ever imagine."

"I looked him up—researched him," I said, voicing a concern I'd been harboring. "There's nothing—no Wikipedia, LinkedIn, or website.

CHAPTER 3

Christ" —my voice rose over the low trumpet solo— "...he doesn't even have a Twitter account."

"He's private."

"Is he old? Ramses was an Egyptian king...right?"

Ross shrugged. "We're not in Egypt and they called them pharaohs. Besides, he's not that old."

My head shook. "Then why is he so secretive? Is he a criminal?"

Ross sat back and stretched his arms over the small table. "I don't give a rat's ass where his money comes from. He reached out to me."

The whole thing gave me the creeps. I looked at my watch, seeing that it was after nine p.m. "Where is he?"

"I don't know, but when someone like Mr. Ramses makes an appointment, we're damn well waiting."

"Fine," I said, standing, my balance a bit off. "I need to order something to eat, or I won't make this meeting."

From the look on Ross's face, he was getting annoyed with me. I didn't care. I was annoyed too. The flight, including a two-hour layover and a mix-up at the hotel, were only a few of my day's highlights. Steadying my footing and wishing I'd not worn a fitted, sleeveless white top that showed a small strip of my midriff, a long flowing skirt, and high-heeled sleek sandals but instead something more practical, I pushed between bodies, making my way to the bar near the rear of the courtyard.

Placing a food order was my immediate goal.

My head buzzed with the sounds as I did my best to avoid the growing number of patrons.

"Excuse me...pardon me."

What legitimate businessman would ask to meet in the courtyard of a dark bar off Canal Street in the French Quarter?

I wedged my way through and up to the bar. "Hey," I yelled to one of the bartenders.

"Just a minute."

Turning, my hand upon the sticky surface, I waited. Blowing my bangs away from my face in the sweltering humidity, I imagined a cool bath back at the hotel. My attention went to the crowd as my skin prickled with that odd sensation of being watched, of wanting to see a familiar face while all the time not wanting to see one.

This was my first trip to New Orleans—other than recently learning this city was where I was born.

I wasn't the daughter of Oliver and Marcella O'Brien. It was after their passing and that of my only brother that I learned I'd been adopted. It was a tremendous jolt to not only lose your parents and sibling, but to learn they were never truly your family.

CHAPTER 3

That didn't mean they hadn't done a good job of raising me and making me feel a part of a family. I only wish they'd told me when I was younger.

Instead of the parentage I'd been led to believe I had, I was in reality the daughter of a woman from New Orleans. Her name was Jezebel North—and from what I'd learned, the name fit. The birth certificate I was shown didn't list a name in the space for father. From what I'd pieced together, the woman who gave birth to me worked in the French Quarter at a private club that was frequented by the dark, dangerous, and powerful people of Louisiana.

To read the speculative tales from nearly thirty years ago, you'd believe in the crime stories of lore.

Jezebel disappeared after giving birth and taking me to the fire station.

The O'Briens raised me in Ashville, within the mountains of North Carolina.

According to those storytellers, New Orleans had changed hands since the men my mother knew were in power. I wasn't referring to elected officials but to the men who took power by force.

To be honest, the story seemed too far-fetched. There were few people in whom I'd confided this information. I turned back to the table, seeing Ross's blond hair.

He was one who knew.

With a shiver, I turned back to the crowd.

From the side of the courtyard, leaning against a stone archway, a strikingly handsome tall man with a dark gaze stared unblinkingly my direction. I turned from side to side, wondering if I was truly who he was looking at.

With broad shoulders that tugged at the seams of his white shirt, he remained still, a statue immune to the influx of patrons. The sleeves of his shirt were rolled up near his elbows, revealing powerful forearms. The top buttons were undone, showing a thick neck. His skin was dark, either tanned from Louisiana sun or perhaps his natural pigment. His dark hair was longer than short and shorter than long. It was combed back in soft waves. Unlike most of the men wearing shorts or blue jeans, this man's long legs were covered with gray dress pants, as if he'd made his way from the business district directly to the happenings of the French Quarter.

"Yeah?" a voice came from the bar.

I spun back, my heartbeat unexpectedly racing and my lips dry. "I'd like to order some food."

The bartender nodded, reaching for a pad of paper.

"I'd like an order of—"

Two large tanned hands and muscular forearms came to either side of me, gripping the bar and caging me. I was trapped between the sticky surface and a solid chest. Heat rose from the ground upward, warming my already-heated skin. The deep voice vibrated his chest as his timbre rumbled through me.

"The lady is mistaken. She's dining with me."

CHAPTER FOUR

I didn't need visual confirmation that the owner of the deep voice was the man from moments ago, the one near the archway. I felt him around me—his presence—as well as within me, confirmed by the way my pulse raced.

I spun within the cage he'd created with his muscular arms.

This man, the one I didn't know, surrounded me, his height dwarfing me and his body electrifying me. The spicy aroma of his cologne mixed with the whiskey on his breath created a concoction that blended perfectly with the Hurricane's rum in my system.

He was so close that at first my eyes met his broad chest. Slowly, I brought my chin higher and higher. His wide neck came into view as his Adam's apple bobbed. Finally, my gaze met his. "I believe you have the wrong—"

The rest of my sentence disappeared into the black hole of his stare.

Such as with a true region in space exhibiting gravitational acceleration so strong that nothing can escape from it, I felt myself drawn into the depth of his nearly black eyes. In the crowded courtyard filled with stagnantly hot, humid New Orleans air, a chill covered my skin, bringing goose bumps to life and drawing my nipples taut.

Why hadn't I worn an outfit with a bra?

What would it feel like to fall into this mountain of a man?

Just another inch forward and my breasts and his chest would collide.

"Our table is waiting, Emma."

Releasing his grip of the bar, the man's large hand came to the small of my back.

My forehead furrowed as I tried to make sense of what made no sense. His touch seemed too intimate and his presumption without merit. "Perhaps I'm the wrong Emma?"

He'd now directed me away from the bar. In his presence, there was no pushing or shoving to get around bodies of other patrons. Instead, the sea of people parted as we walked toward the archway where I'd first seen him.

"No." His deep voice resonated beyond the melancholy music, twisting my insides.

Once out of the courtyard, we entered a dimly lit hallway with flame-like sconces upon the walls. I stopped. "This is ridiculous. I'm not leaving here with you. I don't know you."

His lips quirked as if he found my opposition amusing. "You're quite right, Miss North. We aren't leaving. The owner has graciously provided a private dining room for our enjoyment. And soon we will be well acquainted."

North.

North was not my last name. It was Jezebel's, the woman I'd recently learned gave birth to me.

My neck stiffened. "Sir, you have the wrong Emma. My name is Emma O'Brien."

His strikingly handsome face tilted. "My mistake. I was made aware of the change."

My head shook. "Change? O'Brien isn't a change." I took a step back. "Who are you?"

He reached for my hand, turning my knuckles upward and bending gallantly at the waist, his firm lips brushing over the surface of my skin. Like a match to flint, my hand tingled with the heat brought by his touch. "Please, Emma, call me Rett."

I retrieved my hand. "Rett, your attention is flattering, but I really must go. My friend is waiting."

"No, my dear, Mr. Underwood has gone." He shrugged. "Presumably back to the hotel. Of that I can't be certain. He found...shall we say, a friend?"

My head moved from side to side before I peered over my shoulder toward the courtyard. Down the empty hallway, the music filtered our way as the growing crowd obstructed my view of where Ross had been seated. "He left me?" I turned back to Rett. "Ross wouldn't leave. We had a business meeting."

"About that, let's be seated, and I will fill you in on the particulars."

My feet were still not moving, my high-heel sandals seemingly rooted to the rough tile of the corridor. "You know about our business deal?"

"Emma, I have done my best to learn everything I could about you." His hand again came to my lower back. His fingers splayed warmly upon my skin, between the top and skirt. "Come, let's talk."

"This...it doesn't feel—"

He turned, his one hand skirting my waist while his other, still upon my back, applied pressure. "Come now..." His deep tone echoed through the corridor as his eyes simmered. "Admit to yourself what this does feel like." His possessive hold tightened, bringing me closer. "Admit it is exhilarating and stimulating. Admit that you're curious to hear what I have to say. Admit that you're intrigued and even turned on. When you do, I'll admit my thoughts."

I tried to step away. "You have no right—"

His chin rose, silencing my protest.

I thought back on his last statement as I stared up into his dark orbs. "Your thoughts...about what?"

"Why, about you, of course."

"What about me?"

"Dinner first."

Without provocation, I began to walk in step as Rett led me down the hallway. As he pulled open a heavy wooden door, the floor changed from rough to smooth marble, and we were met with a swoosh of cool air. A smiling woman in a long red gown nodded our way.

Peering down at the top and gauze skirt I'd worn, I suddenly felt significantly underdressed.

"Sir," the lady in red said, "your table is waiting."

As if reading my mind, Rett leaned down, his lips close to my ear as his warm breath teased the sensitive skin of my neck. "You're absolutely spectacular. Your outfit is perfect."

"I-I didn't know..."

Again, he led me as we followed the woman in red.

She opened one of two large wooden doors to an

intimate dining room. The chandelier above acted as a prism, creating golden light that danced upon the ceiling as the crystals swayed. The walls were covered in rich oak paneling, trimmed in intricate carvings. The one and only table was set with a white linen tablecloth and red linen napkins. A single red rose stood in a silver vase with two tall candles in silver holders glowing from the center. Releasing his touch of my back, Rett moved forward and pulled one of the high-backed large chairs away from the table for me to sit.

Once again, I hesitated.

My gaze went to the woman in red. Her equally red lips were curved into a smile, and her eyes were set on me.

Okay. She knew I was here.

That should mean it's safe?

Right?

"Emma."

My name rolled off Rett's tongue with the slightest of accents, deep and commanding, as if giving me little choice but to take the chair he offered.

With a deep breath, I moved forward and sat. Rett pushed the chair toward the table and took the other seat. Seductive music infiltrated the air; unlike the loud notes out in the courtyard, this melody was softer and teamed with the melancholy twang of blues. Even without words, it sounded like poetry floating through the air.

Rett lifted a bottle of wine, presenting the label. "My research showed that you're a connoisseur of red wines, the drier the better."

I didn't speak.

What kind of research had he done?

"This cabernet sauvignon is extremely rare. It's a members-only selection from a quaint vineyard in northern Michigan. I specifically requested it for this evening." Before I could speak, he continued, "The grapes in 2011 were threatened by an early frost. The harvest was expedited, resulting in fewer than one hundred bottles being corked. As you can imagine, acquiring a bottle is not easy."

His dark eyes gleamed with something I couldn't determine.

He continued, "I enjoy the hunt almost as much as the acquisition."

Apparently, the cork had already been removed. Rett poured a small portion into a glass, swirled the contents, and inhaled. "But, my dear Emma, once the target is obtained, rareness alone no longer gives it value. For once it's obtained, the sense of rarity is lost. That is when the true value is tested. That worth comes from the combination of quality, uniqueness, and taste." He passed the glass my way. "Please, have the first sip."

I took the glass. "I already drank a Hurricane. I'm not sure if I should drink any more, especially before food. That was what I was about to do—"

"Only a sip," he interrupted, "and you will understand what I'm saying."

I did as he had, taking the stem in my fingertips and swirling the contents. The aroma filled the globe of the glass, and as the deep ruby liquid stilled, the scents of plum, blackberry, pine, and violets filled my senses. I tipped the glass, allowing the wine to tease my lips. The earlier aromas came to life on my tongue. It truly was unlike any wine I'd ever tasted.

"Well?" he asked.

"It's delicious and you were right, unique."

Rett poured himself a glass and sat back, his button-down white shirt stretching over his wide chest. Against the wide girth of the chair, he appeared almost regal, as if instead of a chair, we were seated in thrones.

"I chose this wine," Rett began, "because of its similarity to you, Emma. Unique, highest quality..." He leaned forward and lifted the glass toward the candlelight. "See how the liquid shimmers?" His dark stare met mine. "It's beautiful like you." He took a sip, his Adam's apple bobbing and the muscles in his neck pulling tight, an involuntary response to the tartness. A grin returned to his full lips. "Pursuing you has been fascinating. I'm aware of your quality and unique nature. Now that you're here, the only parameter yet to decide is taste. However, I have no doubt that you too will taste delicious."

My lungs burned with my caught breath as heat radiated from my cheeks. "That...it's...inappropriate."

His smile returned, this time gleaming from the black holes of his orbs. "No, Emma. It's a perfectly appropriate thing to say to you, the woman who is about to be my wife."

CHAPTER FIVE

My pulse kicked up as Rett's words registered.

Yet how could such a statement truly register?

It was a proclamation with no basis in reality.

Lowering my glass of wine to the linen tablecloth, I laid my hands upon the table's edge, preparing to push my chair away.

"Rett, this—"

The door opened and a second later, a parade of servers entered, thwarting my escape.

Once again, Rett's full lips quirked in amusement, recognizing my failed attempt to flee. Within his dark stare, the reflection of the candles' flames flickered.

"Mr. Ramses," the oldest gentleman in the parade of servers said with a dramatic bow, "we have prepared your meal to your specifications. We do hope that you and your companion will enjoy."

Ramses?

Rett...Everett Ramses.

The connection was made, yet I couldn't speak.

I could—I was capable—it was that Rett was still speaking to the man.

"...thank you, Elijah. I'm sure it will be delicious as usual."

Elijah turned my way and poured more wine into my glass. The other waiters placed plates before us and uncovered dishes of some of New Orleans' traditional delicacies: barbecued shrimp, charbroiled oysters, and golden curry. Their unmistakable aromas swirled through the air, reminding me of my earlier hunger.

"Miss North," Elijah said, "Mr. Ramses said it had been a while since you visited your home. Please let us know if we can bring you anything that isn't offered."

I inhaled, looking from Elijah to Rett.

I wanted to say that I could be offered my real name—O'Brien. I wanted to say that New Orleans wasn't my home. Pittsburgh was where I'd called home since graduating from college.

However, it was clear that to do so would prolong

this conversation. Therefore, I simply said, "Thank you, Elijah."

By the time Rett and I were once again alone, the servers had heaped generous portions of each dish upon our plates. As close as I'd been to making an escape, the delicious aromas were making my stomach growl.

After the door closed, Rett looked my way. "Eat, Emma. You yourself said you were famished."

"I was expecting French fries or onion rings, not a seafood smorgasbord." I lay the spoon down that I had just lifted. "You're Everett Ramses."

He nodded. "I am."

"Why do you keep referring to me as North when my name is O'Brien?"

"We will get to that."

My head shook. "Okay, so you're Everett Ramses, and that's how you knew about the business meeting."

"Correct," he said, drizzling lemon juice over an oyster before sliding it from its shell onto a thin cracker and eating it.

I stared for a minute, my gaze volleying between the man at the end of the table and my still-untouched food.

How did I get here...to a private dining room with him, the man Ross has been talking about nonstop?

The only one who could answer my question was Ross.

I pushed my chair away from the table and stood. "Thank you for the invitation. I must bid you goodbye, Mr. Ramses. This has been...interesting; however, I believe—"

Before I could finish my sentence, Rett was out of his seat and in front of me.

Perhaps it was the length of his legs or maybe he had been a track star in an earlier life. I wasn't certain how he'd moved as quickly and yet as gracefully as he did. Much like a panther threatening its prey, Rett had me blocked. The door was beyond him.

I took a step to the side and then another in the other direction. Forward wasn't an option.

I sucked in a breath as my neck and shoulders straightened.

Instead of toward the door, I stepped backward—the two of us moving in sync—away from my escape. Our unchoreographed dance continued until my shoulders collided with the wall, and I was sandwiched between the carved-wood paneling and over six feet of solid man.

"Emma, you don't understand."

My breathing quickened, yet I wasn't inhaling, not in a way that brought the needed oxygen to my rushing bloodstream. The result was a tingling in my extremities.

Rett—no, Mr. Ramses—was so close.

I inhaled the mix of garlic and wine on his warm breath, as well as his rich, spicy cologne. Warmth radiated from his solid body. I placed my palms against his chest, feeling the rhythm of his heart beneath. My head shook. "I don't. You're right. I don't understand—any of this."

Reaching for my hands before a protest came to my lips, he lifted both of them over my head, pinning them to the wall. The move caused my back to arch, pushing my breasts forward. He stared, scanning me down and back up. No longer did the candles flicker in the dark orbs, but something more unnerving. As his gaze lingered, physical changes occurred within me. My insides twisted, no longer from hunger for food, but with an appetite for something I shouldn't want.

What is it about this man that speaks to me, not with his voice but with his mere presence?

Never in my life had I felt such an attraction, as if I wasn't in control of my body's reactions. I'd turned down men like him in the past, men who oozed power and dominance. I'd walked away with my head held high. And yet with Rett, in a matter of maybe an hour, I was putty in his hands.

It was more than the way he commanded the situation; it was also the lustful desire in his eyes. I saw it in his stare, the way the dark now swirled with more. The throbbing of my core caused my high heels to shift upon the floor as my desire grew.

As he leaned closer, I knew for sure that it wasn't just me.

A hardening erection against my tummy alerted me that he wanted me as much as I wanted him.

Holding my hands in place above my head with one hand, Rett teased a stray strand of my golden hair away from my cheek with his other. He then traced my lower lip with his thumb. A tug and my mouth opened with a soft *pop*. Without instruction, I allowed his thumb to enter. Closing my lips, I sucked, tasting the saltiness of his oyster.

My eyes fluttered shut as a moan bubbled within me. It was as I opened my eyes that I saw it. Similar to a spark to dry kindling, what had previously been flickers in his eyes had combusted to a raging fire.

Rett removed his thumb, again tracing my lip. "Emma, the business deal is complete. Your little project is funded."

His proximity and the way he was touching me had me distracted, but I knew what he was saying deserved my attention. "It is? You agreed to partner—"

CHAPTER 5

He held my lips with the pressure of his finger, stopping my question and interrupting. "I didn't agree to be a partner."

My breasts heaved as he leaned closer, his rigid, toned body pressing me tighter against the wall. The pressure painfully stretched my upheld arms, while at the same time, Rett wordlessly informed me by the rock hardness of his erection that I was truly desired.

"I agreed to a deal," he said definitively.

CHAPTER SIX

Rett's deep voice had my full attention. "I was contacted a while ago, informed of your true identity."

My head shook. "I'm who I am. Emma O'Brien is my identity."

"You are correct. However, Miss North, you are more important than that. Your biological father was my father's greatest adversary. They were each involved in the other's demise. New Orleans is now mine, and who better to be at my side than the daughter of Isaiah Boudreau?"

Isaiah Boudreau.

I'd never heard that name.

My head shook. "I don't know him or you."

Again, Rett traced my lips as his chest flattened

my breasts, and his hips pushed closer. "Fight me, Emma. Tell me you don't want me."

I pulled against his grip, yet I didn't have the strength to break it. The undeniable truth, evident by the warmth pooling between my thighs and dampening my panties, my nipples tightening, and my breasts becoming heavy with need, was that I didn't want to fight.

I wanted him too. Instead of replying, I asked, "Rett, what deal did you make?"

His stare bore into me, heating me from within. The tepid coolness of the air conditioning disappeared as the temperature rose.

"I traded the investment for something I desired more than a piece of an insignificant software program."

This time I gave it effort, fighting his grip. "Our work is *not* insignificant."

Rett's grin returned, a bit more sinister than before. "Easy, tiger. Do not take offense. You see" — he was still holding my wrists— "...everything is insignificant in comparison."

"What is this thing of great value that you want?"

"Who." He leaned down, bringing his firm lips to mine.

I didn't fight, not to get away.

Maybe I'd been drugged, or perhaps it was

CHAPTER 6

Everett Ramses who had me intoxicated. Whatever the case, in his presence I wasn't thinking straight. As his kiss deepened, the air filled with moans and whimpers.

Were they from me?

I pulled at his grip, wanting my hands free. I needed to touch him as his free hand was touching me, fingers splayed over my back, coming forward and caressing my breasts. Under my top, he tweaked my diamond-hard nipples as energy zapped from his touch to my twisting core.

Multitalented, he was competent in more than caresses as he held me captive. Simultaneously, his tongue teased the seam of my lips. I'd lost the will to protest, opening and welcoming his unique taste, like that of the wine.

Rett pulled away as I gasped for breath. His dark stare focused on mine. "Are you wet, Emma?"

His question seemed too personal, but then again, if I was, he was the cause. "Yes," I panted.

Releasing my hands, he grinned, taking a step back. "Lift your skirt. I want to see for myself."

I couldn't move my gaze away from his even if I wanted it to. "Rett, please."

His large hand reached for my chin. "Listen carefully, sweet Emma. The deal is done. You're now mine. As mine, you will be pampered beyond your wildest imagination. The world is yours. I will lay the heads of your enemies at your feet and indulge your every desire. Your one task is to be mine, ready for me and willing to obey whatever I ask."

My eyes opened wider and my breathing quickened as he continued.

Obey.

Who used words like that in today's world?

"What...?"

"You will fall to your knees or spread your sexy legs when I command. You will submit to me when and where I want. That is nonnegotiable. And you will do whatever I demand willingly because when you do, you will be rewarded with earthshaking orgasms, the greatest of your life—because I promise that with me, you will come over and over."

He was wrong. I wasn't a multiple-orgasm woman. One and done.

"Rett—"

His finger upon my lips again stopped my words.

"There is one more nonnegotiable requirement: you will take my name, marry me."

My skirt was in my grasp. With each of his declarations, I'd balled the material higher and higher until it was a soft roll above my waist, showing my black lace panties, bare legs, and high heels.

CHAPTER 6

Rett took a step back, scanning the lace. "Touch yourself."

Heat slid up my neck to my cheeks, no doubt bringing a glow of pink to my skin.

"Oh, my little Emma, now is not the time to be bashful. Did you not hear what I just said?"

Biting my lip, I nodded and peered about.

This dining room was private, but how private?

Before I could voice my concern, Rett continued, his deep voice commanding my attention. "My request is not the issue. It could have been for you to bend over the table, flatten your breasts, and bare your perfect round ass to me. No matter the request, what matters is your immediate obedience. Quite simply put, you will do as I say and be rewarded or hesitate and be punished. I'm not a man who repeats himself."

I couldn't describe what had come over me since meeting this man, other than an overwhelming mixture of shock, yearning, and desire. The idea of punishment at his hands didn't deter me. I wasn't afraid of him, and yet I had an unmistakable desire to please him.

My hand slid under the waistband of my panties as my legs parted. A small whimper escaped my lips as I found my own damp core.

"Show me." His tenor had dropped from

moments ago, now ladened with the huskiness of lust.

I pulled my hand out of the confines of my panties.

Rett reached for it, lifting my fingers to his lips and sucking. His cheeks rose and a grin formed. "Delicious, as I suspected."

Before I could form a response, he was kneeling before me, removing my panties as his warm breath skirted my sensitive skin. My gaze darted to the door, afraid the servers would return, when all at once, his mouth covered my core, his teeth nipping my swollen clit and his tongue delving within me.

"Oh," I cried out, my hands going to his dark hair, weaving my fingers through his mane for support as more sounds and indistinguishable words filled the air. I let out a gust of air as an orgasm threatened to double me forward. Such as a freight train barreling through a dark night, the overwhelming explosion came over me suddenly and without warning.

Though I'd come, Rett didn't stop. It was clear that he too had been starving, and I was his feast. My mind remembered I didn't have multiple orgasms, but my body was a different story. Ravenously he nibbled and sucked. His hands held to my behind, pulling me closer.

The second orgasm was stronger than the first.

CHAPTER 6

I called out his name—Rett—this man I barely knew.

My body trembled with the aftershocks as I struggled for breath on weakened knees. Rett stood, allowing my skirt to cascade to my ankles before scooping me into his arms, cradling me against his solid chest, and taking me back to the chair where I had been seated. When our eyes met, I bashfully asked, "My panties?"

"No. I want you bare and available to me at all times."

I nodded.

It wasn't a confirmation of my acceptance as much as my acknowledgment that he'd spoken.

With a chaste kiss, one that left my own essence on my lips, Rett pushed the chair back to the table and returned to his seat.

My hands shook as I reached for my glass of wine. The red liquid quivered as I brought the glass to my lips. After consuming a generous portion, I stared beyond the candles to the man now casually dining upon his meal. A forkful of shrimp and an oyster on a cracker—it was as if we hadn't just...My head shook as I found my voice. "Let me get this straight. Ross made you a deal regarding me?"

"No."

"No?"

Rett dabbed the napkin at the corner of his lips, the same lips that had just brought me to ecstasy—twice.

"After both an in-depth conversation with your friend and my own diligent research, I contacted Mr. Underwood again and offered him a deal he couldn't refuse."

My head shook. "You can't make deals regarding people. It doesn't work like that."

Amusement again danced in his dark orbs. "My dear, the deal is done."

"Why do you think I'd go along with this?"

Lowering his fork to the plate before him, Rett sat taller and took a breath. "You are a marked woman."

I had to wonder if he was referring to what we'd just done.

Everett Ramses went on. "Your brother wants you dead."

I sat straighter. "Kyle died in the accident with our parents. He's been gone for over four years."

"No, my dear, Kyle O'Brien is very much alive. He's bided his time and now believes he can claim New Orleans. However, to achieve his goal, he must overcome two obstacles."

"Two?"

CHAPTER 6

"Me," Rett said, leaning back in his throne-like chair and reaching for the arms, "and you."

"What do I have to do with any of this?"

"Kyle, your adopted brother, is claiming that his stake to the city rests on the notion that he is the child Jezebel North gave up. You see, he's proclaiming that he is the true heir of Isaiah Boudreau."

The reality of Rett's words settled around me in a fog.

"My brother is alive and wants me dead?"

"He knows you're here, in New Orleans."

"What does that mean?"

"It means you will stay with me. I will protect you, and once you're legally Emma Ramses, you will be untouchable."

I stood, no longer able to sit still. Cool air flowed under my skirt, a reminder I was nude beneath.

"This is ludicrous. I should just go back to Pittsburgh."

"No," Rett said definitively. "I have had you under protection there since I first learned."

"There were people watching me?"

"That is done. Your home is in New Orleans."

My hands went out, coming back to slap my thighs. "And do what, Rett? My life is in Pittsburgh."

"Your education and dream is to be a writer.

There is no better place in the world than here, but most importantly, you will be my wife." When I didn't respond, he went on, "I have men waiting to escort us away from this restaurant."

"Away, to where?" I asked.

"To my home. It's very safe."

My gaze darted to the door and back. "And if I say no? If I just leave?"

Rett gestured toward the door. "You won't, but as you are my future wife, I prefer not to hold you captive against your will." He shrugged. "I will, but I'd prefer you cooperate."

I tugged at my lip with my teeth as I contemplated all that had been said. "What will happen if I leave?"

"If you walk through that door alone, you will be vulnerable, not only to Kyle but also to his men. You may succeed in making it to the courtyard or possibly the sidewalk beyond; however, I can unequivocally say that...one more step would mean certain death."

∽

Thank you for reading "FATE'S DEMAND" by Aleatha Romig. She enjoyed writing this sexy, dark, romantic short story for the anthology *ONE MORE*

STEP entitled "THE DEAL" as a showcase for her writing style.

If you enjoyed this short story about Rett and Emma, the setting of New Orleans, the power of a man like Everett Ramses, the strength of a woman like Emma, and their instant chemistry be sure to find out what happens next in *DEVIL'S DEAL*.

Pre-order your copy by clicking on the link. And for a sneak peek, turn the page.

DEVIL'S DEAL

By:
ALEATHA ROMIG

Emma

Rett gestured toward the door I'd just threatened to leave. "You won't," he said, "but as you are my future wife, I prefer not to hold you captive against your will." He shrugged. "I will, but I'd prefer you cooperate."

The sound of Rett's deep voice combined with his New Orleans draw rattled through my mind. His dark stare met mine even as my eyes closed. My pulse raced with the memories of what he'd done, what I'd allowed him to do to me. Lingering in a place between pleasure and pain, my core remained twisted with the understanding that in a matter of a few hours or less, I'd put aside all I'd known—all that I had heard with my own ears and seen with my own eyes—for the words, no, for the demand of a man who somehow scattered both my body and mind.

It was too much. I couldn't concentrate.

Much like driving on a dark night through a downpour, searching for an unknown street sign with the radio turned up, the driver reached for the volume and turned down the familiar song. It didn't lessen the falling rain, bring sunlight to the night sky, or make the sign more visible; it simply reduced the stimuli.

That was what I sought as Everett Ramses's demand lingered in the air, mixing with the concoction of the delicious aromas from the seafood smorgasbord, the remaining alcohol circulating through my bloodstream, and the dampness he'd facilitated between my thighs.

"Why should I believe you?" I asked.

"Because you know I'm right."

His response was simple and while ridiculous, there was a part of me, deep inside, that wondered if he could be right—was right.

Rett stood, pushing back the throne-like chair from where he'd made his decrees. My breathing hitched as with each stride he came closer. There was no need to rush, he knew his audience was captive, not as captive as I would be, but still, my high heels were rooted to the floor as I gripped the chair before me. The seams of his white shirt pulled with his deep breaths. His handsome face showed no signs of emotion.

The enticing cloud surrounding him added to the overwhelming assault on my mind. Wine, seafood, and rich, spicy cologne filled my senses as he pulled out my chair and encouraged me to sit.

"You see," he said as I sat and he stayed behind me. His slick timbre sliced through the air. "You know that what I've said is true."

Before I could speak, his large hands skirted up my arms.

They were the only part of him that I could see, yet I felt him behind me, his presence dominating my thoughts, settling the chaos as I concentrated only on him. Closing my eyes, I let his deep rumblings infiltrate my mind, setting off reactions within me; much like the silver ball within an old-fashioned pinball machine, they ricocheted from here to there.

The warmth of his touch moved higher.

"Think about it, Emma. The times you wondered if by chance you left your door unlocked. The sounds you heard in the middle of the night. The times you walked along a dark sidewalk, your senses on high alert as you looked left and then right, wondering if you were being watched. And the instances when you wondered if things were out of place, knowing they shouldn't be but having a feeling, one you couldn't shake."

Despite his warm touch, my skin cooled. With each of his phrases, I recalled an instance or maybe more. I was so lost in my thoughts that I hadn't realized where his hands had landed, what they were doing, until the pressure on my neck became uncomfortable.

"Your life has been in my hands, as it is now."

Alarm sent adrenaline through my circulation as I reached up, tugging and prying at his fingers. Though my painted nails scratched, his grip didn't cease.

"You would be dead if it weren't for me."

Was I to die tonight?

He squeezed tighter. "Are you frightened?"

My lungs burned as I fought to fill them with air. I didn't or couldn't answer.

"Let it not be said, Emma, that I didn't give you a choice. Your choice is right here, right now. It's me or death." Rett's grip intensified as the pressure on my neck increased. His lips came close to my ear, warm air teasing my oversensitive skin. "I made myself a promise. If you chose death, it would be at my hands."

The panic that had been building within me evaporated into the humid New Orleans breeze blowing beyond the walls. Despite Rett's grasp, the dark spots dancing before my eyes, and the burning in my chest, I had a sudden realization, perhaps an epiphany. I dropped my hands to my lap, no longer fighting Rett's threat.

My reaction, or lack of one, had the response I'd expected—the response that I'd bet my life on.

Rett released my neck.

I couldn't help but gasp as air rushed into my lungs. It was similar to coming out of the water after diving into the deep end of the pool. As air filled me, my senses were turned up. Not only the aromas but everything—touch, sight, hearing, and taste.

The soft jazz music coming from the hidden speakers was louder and the flickering candles were brighter. The world spun, not metaphorically. Rett turned the chair where I was seated toward him. With his tight grip now on the arms of the chair, he leaned forward until his dark stare was inches away from mine. With my complete attention, he questioned, "Are you submitting to death?"

"No." My voice was a bit scratchy. I tried to even my breathing, confident in my next statement. "You won't hurt me."

The expression before me morphed as this handsome man took on a villainous grin. "Are you certain, Miss North?"

First, my name wasn't North. However, with each passing beat of my heart, I was certain of my statement. I was confident that if Everett Ramses wanted me dead, he wouldn't have pledged his protection even before I knew his name. If he wanted me dead, he could have very easily squeezed my last breath as his strong fingers crushed my neck, my larynx, and trachea until I could no longer inhale.

I lifted my chin. "Yes, I'm certain."

Rett stood erect, his penetrating stare still on me. "You're wrong."

Reaching for the edge of the table and pushing the large chair back, I stood, keeping my gaze fixed on his. If this was a contest on who would blink first, I was giving it my best damn shot. "If I'm to believe you, Mr. Ramses, you have been protecting me from an unknown threat." I grinned. "Are you saying you're not to be believed?"

Almost unperceivable to the eye, his head shook. Such a micro-reaction was the telltale sign that Everett Ramses was a man who rarely showed his hand. He kept his emotions and intentions close to the vest. And yet, a moment before, despite his tenor and the equal cadence of his words, he'd been pushed to his limit, showing me his true feelings. No, Everett Ramses didn't want me dead.

"Miss North, it isn't a lie when I say, I could easily extinguish that glowing ember in your blue eyes. I'm a man of my word, and I meant what I said. You will be protected from your brother as well as other forces working against you." He lifted his chin. "With one exception."

"What would that be?"

"Not what, who." He inhaled, his nostrils flaring as he scanned me up and down. "Me, Emma. I won't make promises I can't keep. I won't pledge not to hurt you. I'm not an easy man. Marrying me will save you from your brother, but not from me." Like lasers, his dark eyes scanned the neckline of my blouse. "You'll pay for my name and my protection.

"Pay?"

"With your loyalty and obedience. I told you before that obeying will bring you rewards."

He'd said orgasms, but I wasn't ready to interrupt him.

"Disobeying will result in punishment."

"Mr. Ramses, I'm not a child."

Rett seized my hand and tugged me forward until it was trapped between his grasp and his rock-hard erection, not so hidden beneath his expensive gray pants. "Do you feel what you do to me?"

My pulse increased. "Yes."

"I'm well aware that you're not a child, Emma. Children don't make me hard. I want a woman, a mature, sensual, and strong woman. Don't act like a child, and I won't treat you like one. Your job from this day forward is simple. Act like the woman capable of being my wife. Show the world that you were born to be the queen of New Orleans. As I said, that will make you untouchable, to everyone except to me." He pressed my hand harder against him. "I will touch you, Emma. Every inch of that soft skin will be mine for the taking. Just like my lips and tongue brought you pleasure, my cock will find pleasure inside you. I'll show you how a woman should be treated. With me, in my bed or wherever I choose, you'll find more pleasure than you knew possible."

With just his words, I was ready to combust, and after what had occurred earlier, I couldn't possibly argue the accuracy in his promise.

"But that doesn't mean I'll spare you pain. You, Emma North, will learn how to enjoy both." Releasing my hand, he continued, "Time is of the essence. Kyle's proximity is closer than I like. You asked what would happen if you left this room." His head shook. "I won't allow you to leave unaccompanied and end up in the hands of the man you considered your brother." He reached for my chin. "Listen to me."

This touch was different than seconds earlier. Everett Ramses may think he was a master at controlling his emotions, yet I saw the restraint in his expression. This touch was gentler, even sensual. The contrast from seconds before sent shock waves over my skin and through my circulation. It wasn't the wine that left me intoxicated as much as it was this man filled with mystery and a kaleidoscope of intense emotion.

"You're mine, Emma. Our union and marriage is what's best for New Orleans. It's also what is best for you; however, you should know that if the time comes when you change your mind and you choose death, it will be at my hands. What is your choice?"

Who would willingly choose death?

I lifted my palm to Rett's chest, splaying my fingers over the shirt. Beneath my touch, his heart beat a steady yet fast rhythm. For only a moment, I let myself gather strength. "Tonight, my choice is you, Everett Ramses." I tilted my head to the side. "I'm willing to see where fate leads. Just know, I'm not easily intimidated. Don't underestimate me. While I'm intrigued by you, I'm not a fragile flower you're saving from wilting. I can handle whatever you throw my way.

"However, you should know that just because you make me wet and are capable of providing my body pleasure doesn't mean you'll ever have my heart. I locked that away years ago. You decide, Mr. Ramses, is this still a deal you want?"

His arm wrapped around my waist, pulling my hips to his, his erection prodding my stomach as my neck craned upward. "I never offered love, Emma. This agreement is what fate demands of us both. It's a deal for my city and for your life. Love is a weakness, an Achilles' heel, so to speak. It's better that we both understand the limitations of our agreement from the start. My offer is for my name and my protection. Hearts are only useful to circulate oxygen through our bloodstream. Marry me and yours will keep beating. I have no other use for it."

Inhaling, I took in Rett's face. There was no question that he was handsome with his defined chin, his high cheekbones, and his protruding brow over his intensely dark eyes. The dark hair on his head was still mussed from where I'd woven my fingers through it as he brought me to ecstasy—twice. I found the man enticing and attractive.

Did that mean he was a good man? A kind man? A man I could love?

Those answers didn't matter. Love wasn't something that either of us sought.

Rett was asking for a commitment—a promise—to a legal agreement, one that I was certain would bring me pleasure in ways only this man could give. It wasn't as if he wanted my heart and soul. They weren't even mine to give. He'd never know why. It wasn't his business.

This agreement was to fulfill fate's demand. I could do that. A smile came to my lips. "I agree, for today."

"No, Emma, till death us do part."

Don't miss this exciting romantic suspense with all the Aleatha twists and turns guaranteed to keep you turning pages late into the night.

Pre-order Devil's Deal today.

WHAT TO DO NOW

LEND IT: Did you enjoy FATE'S DEMAND? Do you have a friend who'd enjoy FATE'S DEMAND? FATE'S DEMAND may be lent one time. Sharing is caring!

RECOMMEND IT: Do you have multiple friends who'd enjoy my dark romance with twists and turns and an all new sexy and infuriating anti-hero? Tell them about it! Call, text, post, tweet...your recommendation is the nicest gift you can give to an author!

REVIEW IT: Tell the world. Please go to the retailer where you purchased this book, as well as Goodreads, and write a review. Please share your thoughts about FATE'S DEMAND on:

*Amazon, FATE'S DEMAND Customer Reviews

*Barnes & Noble, FATE'S DEMAND, Customer Reviews

*iBooks, FATE'S DEMAND Customer Reviews

* BookBub, FATE'S DEMAND Customer Reviews

*Goodreads.com/Aleatha Romig

BOOKS BY NEW YORK TIMES
BESTSELLING AUTHOR ALEATHA ROMIG

NEW STORY COMING:

DEVIL'S DEAL

Coming May 2121

THE SPARROW WEBS:

DANGEROUS WEB:

DUSK

Releasing Nov, 2020

DARK

Releasing 2021

DAWN

Releasing 2021

WEB OF DESIRE:

SPARK

Released Jan. 14, 2020

FLAME

Released February 25, 2020

ASHES

Released April 7, 2020

TANGLED WEB:

TWISTED

Released May, 2019

OBSESSED

Released July, 2019

BOUND

Released August, 2019

WEB OF SIN:

SECRETS

Released October, 2018

LIES

Released December, 2018

PROMISES

Released January, 2019

∽

THE INFIDELITY SERIES:

BETRAYAL

Book #1

Released October 2015

CUNNING

Book #2

Released January 2016

DECEPTION

Book #3

Released May 2016

ENTRAPMENT

Book #4

Released September 2016

FIDELITY

Book #5

Released January 2017

∾

THE CONSEQUENCES SERIES:

CONSEQUENCES

(Book #1)

Released August 2011

TRUTH

(Book #2)

Released October 2012

CONVICTED

(Book #3)

Released October 2013

REVEALED

(Book #4)

Previously titled: Behind His Eyes Convicted: The Missing Years

Re-released June 2014

BEYOND THE CONSEQUENCES

(Book #5)

Released January 2015

RIPPLES

Released October 2017

CONSEQUENCES COMPANION READS:

BEHIND HIS EYES-CONSEQUENCES

Released January 2014

BEHIND HIS EYES-TRUTH

Released March 2014

∾

STAND ALONE MAFIA THRILLER:

PRICE OF HONOR

Available Now

∾

THE LIGHT DUET:

Published through Thomas and Mercer Amazon exclusive

INTO THE LIGHT

Released June, 2016

AWAY FROM THE DARK

Released October, 2016

TALES FROM THE DARK SIDE SERIES:

INSIDIOUS

(All books in this series are stand-alone erotic thrillers)

Released October 2014

ALEATHA'S LIGHTER ONES:

PLUS ONE

Stand-alone fun, sexy romance

May 2017

ANOTHER ONE

Stand-alone fun, sexy romance

May 2018

ONE NIGHT

Stand-alone, sexy contemporary romance

September 2017

A SECRET ONE

April 2018

INDULGENCE SERIES:

UNEXPECTED

Released August, 2018

UNCONVENTIONAL

Released January, 2018

UNFORGETTABLE

Released October, 2019

UNDENIABLE

Released August, 2020

ABOUT THE AUTHOR

Aleatha Romig is a New York Times, Wall Street Journal, and USA Today bestselling author who lives in Indiana, USA. She has raised three children with her high school sweetheart and husband of over thirty years. Before she became a full-time author, she worked days as a dental hygienist and spent her nights writing. Now, when she's not imagining mind-blowing twists and turns, she likes to spend her time with her family and friends. Her other pastimes include reading and creating heroes/anti-heroes who haunt your dreams!

Aleatha impresses with her versatility in writing. She released her first novel, CONSEQUENCES, in August of 2011. CONSEQUENCES, a dark romance, became a bestselling series with five novels and two companions released from 2011 through 2015. The compelling and epic story of Anthony and Claire Rawlings has graced more than half a million e-readers. Her first stand-alone smart, sexy thriller INSIDIOUS was next. Then Aleatha released the five-novel

INFIDELITY series, a romantic suspense saga, that took the reading world by storm, the final book landing on three of the top bestseller lists. She ventured into traditional publishing with Thomas and Mercer. Her books INTO THE LIGHT and AWAY FROM THE DARK were published through this mystery/thriller publisher in 2016. In the spring of 2017, Aleatha again ventured into a different genre with her first fun and sexy stand-alone romantic comedy with the USA Today bestseller PLUS ONE. She continued with ONE NIGHT and ANOTHER ONE. If you like fun, sexy, novellas that make your heart pound, try her UNCONVENTIONAL and UNEXPECTED. In 2018 Aleatha returned to her dark romance roots with SPARROW WEBS.

Aleatha is a "Published Author's Network" member of the Romance Writers of America and PEN America. She is represented by Kevan Lyon of Marsal Lyon Literary Agency and Dani Sanchez with Wildfire Marketing.

facebook.com/aleatharomig
twitter.com/aleatharomig
instagram.com/aleatharomig

Made in United States
North Haven, CT
18 July 2022

21509623R00048